HOT SHOT

THE #1
SPORTS SERIES
FOR KIDS

HOT SHOT

LITTLE, BROWN AND COMPANY
NEW YORK • BOSTON

Little, Brown Books for Young Readers

Hachette Book Group
237 Park Avenue, New York, NY 10017
Visit our Web site at www.lb-kids.com

www.mattchristopher.com

Little, Brown Books for Young Readers is a division of Hachette Book
Group, Inc. The Little, Brown name and logo are trademarks of
Hachette Book Group, Inc.

First Edition: February 2010

Peters, Stephanie True, 1965–
    Hot shot / [text written by Stephanie True Peters]. — 1st ed.
        p. cm.
    "Matt Christopher, the #1 sports series for kids."
    Summary: Thirteen-year-old Julian Pryce was star center on an
undefeated basketball team before moving to a new town, where he
quickly gets on the wrong side of the starting center, whose father
happens to be their coach.
    ISBN 978-0-316-04482-0
    [1. Basketball — Fiction.   2. Coaching (Athletics) — Fiction.
3. Moving, Household — Fiction.   4. Egoism — Fiction.   5. Teamwork
(Sports) — Fiction.]   I. Title
    PZ7.P441833Hot2010
    [Fic] — dc22
                                                            2009006788

10 9 8 7 6 5 4 3 2 1

Text written by Stephanie True Peters

CW

Printed in the United States of America

HOT SHOT

1

Julian Pryce sat on the bench in the gym. His head was bowed. His hands dangled between his knees.

Something bad was about to happen. He alone knew what it was. He'd known it for almost a month, actually. He wished he could do something to stop it. But he couldn't. It was out of his control.

The coach of the Tornadoes basketball team, Mr. Valenti, strode into the gym. "Good afternoon, boys. Before we begin, I have an announcement."

Here it comes, Julian thought. His heart started to thrum in his chest.

"I'm sorry to have to tell you this," the coach said, "but this is Julian's last game with us."

Julian stared at the floor, listening to his teammates gasp.

"What do you mean, this is his last game? Did he —

Julian, are you quitting or something?" The question came from Cal, the second string center.

Julian's head shot up. "No! I'm not a quitter!"

"Julian's family is moving on Saturday," the coach said quietly.

"What?!" Grady Coughlin, one of Julian's best friends, grabbed him by the arm. "You're *moving*? Since when?"

"Since my dad got a promotion last month," Julian said miserably.

"Why didn't you tell me? Tell us?" Grady cried.

Julian scrubbed his hands over his face. "I don't know! Maybe because saying it out loud would make it real. Or because I didn't want to go through an awkward good-bye. Or maybe because I figured that you all would start treating me differently."

"Treating you differently?" Grady echoed. "Like how?"

Julian sighed. "Like since I was moving, maybe it didn't make sense to include me in stuff you were doing. Why bother with me if I was leaving, you know?"

Grady pushed his straight blond hair away from his forehead and gave Julian a long look. Then he nodded solemnly. "Yeah, I see what you're saying. And you're right. I would have totally ignored you."

2

Julian blinked. "You — really?"

Grady's serious look changed into a broad smile. "Uh, *no*! Sheesh, man, what kind of friend do you think I am?" He kicked Julian lightly in the shin.

Julian barely felt it. He was too busy feeling something else — relief! That feeling grew even greater as his teammates gathered around him, patting him on the back, socking him in the arm, and telling him what an idiot he was for even thinking that way.

Coach Valenti clapped his hands. "All right, now that the bad news is out of the way, what do you say we start with the layup drill? The other team is going to be here soon and we want to be sure we're warmed up."

"Yeah, but we're not going to be warmed up, Coach," forward Mick Reiss interjected. "We're going to be *red hot*!"

The team exploded in shouts of agreement. Then they split into two lines at mid-court and took turns going to the basket for layups and retrieving the shots.

Julian was the third player to shoot. Unlike some taller-than-average thirteen-year-olds, he had a steady, controlled dribble. He also had a great shooting touch. Now, as he neared the basket, he gently guided the ball up to the sweet spot on the backboard. It hit perfectly and fell through the net with a soft swishing sound. Cal nabbed the ball and then he and Julian switched lines.

Julian watched his teammates move through the drill. He marveled at how smoothly they worked together. It hadn't always been that way. In fact, at the beginning of the season, they'd looked so clumsy that Julian had almost given up hope of winning a single game.

Losing wasn't something Julian was used to. Last season, he'd been the star center of the undefeated Tornadoes. As the team's high scorer and top rebounder, he'd been featured in the local newspaper many times. The walls of his bedroom were covered with framed articles and photos. His shelves held several trophies, too, including a big one for winning the tournament championship.

Of course, he hadn't won all those games or the championship single-handedly. His teammates had contributed just as much.

That's why he'd gotten such a shock at the start of this season. He'd hurried eagerly into the gym. He expected to see a few familiar faces from the previous year's starting lineup. Instead, he learned that he was the only starter returning!

Art and Danny were both a year older and had moved up to the next division. Max had moved out of town. And Barry Streeter, an outstanding forward, had been in a terrible car accident just the day before. He was seriously injured, possibly even crippled for life.

Julian had been horrified to hear of the accident. He couldn't imagine Barry lying in bed unable to move.

But he was also troubled by the fact that his new teammates seemed to expect him to shoulder the role of team leader. Being the team leader would be great if they won games. But if they lost, he'd be blamed. When he saw how poorly the Tornadoes performed that first practice, he knew he didn't want that responsibility.

That's when he started showing up late to practice, giving less than 100 percent on the court, and turning away whenever his teammates tried to include him in activities outside of practice.

Then he visited Barry in the hospital. He started to complain about how lousy the team was and how he wasn't sure he wanted to be a part of it anymore. Barry listened for a few minutes and then asked him a simple question: "How'd you like to switch places?"

The question humbled Julian. He realized Barry would've given *anything* to be on the court instead of in that hospital cot. From there on out, he had stopped taking basketball, and his teammates, for granted, and started giving his all to the Tornadoes again — even after his father announced that they would be moving.

"Julian, you're up!"

The call startled Julian back to the present. Cal was already dribbling the ball toward the hoop for his layup. Julian took off at a fast trot. As he leaped to capture the rebound, something suddenly occurred to him.

This is the last time I'll do this drill with these guys!

2

This is the last time . . .

That same phrase repeated itself in Julian's mind when his teammates put their hands together before the game.

This is the last time I'll yell for Tornadoes to win.

He thought it when he stood in the mid-court circle with Grady and Len, Mick and Terrell, for the opening tip-off.

This is the last time I'll stand in this spot wearing this uniform.

But then that thought, and all others that didn't have to do with the game, fled. It was time to play ball!

The Tornadoes were facing the Jets. Julian recognized the other center from last year. Back then, he'd had no trouble winning the tip because he'd towered over his opponent.

But what a difference a year had made! He and the Jet now stood eye to eye, and unless he was wrong . . .

The kid has facial hair! Yikes!

The referee stepped into the circle and held a basketball between the two centers. He gave a blast on his whistle and tossed the ball straight up.

Julian and the other center leaped, arms stretched high. For a split second, Julian thought the Jet was going to touch the ball first. But somehow, he got his fingers on it and with a decisive tap, sent it zipping down to Grady's waiting hands.

Grady dribbled forward. A Jet player shadowed him. Grady held out his left arm to shield the ball as he moved toward the right-side baseline corner.

The Jet put on the pressure, pushing Grady farther to the sideline and away from the hoop. A few more steps and Grady would wind up trapped in the corner!

But Grady surprised the Jet. He stopped short, still dribbling, threw a head-fake, and then passed the ball behind his back to his other hand! Now dribbling lefty, he dashed back to the top of the key.

The Jet fell for the maneuver hook, line, and sinker. Grady, meanwhile, sent the ball to Mick, playing forward. Mick dribbled into the key and glanced at Julian. For a moment, Julian thought he was going to pass to him. But then the tall Jet center darted between them. So Mick lofted a jump shot from six feet away instead.

The ball banked off the backboard, hit the rim, and rolled once around the hoop before finally dropping in. The Tornadoes were on the scoreboard!

They didn't stop to cheer, however, for the Jets were already preparing to inbound the ball.

"Defense!" Julian cried. "Get into the zone!"

Coach Valenti rotated his team through three different zone defenses each game. There was one-three-one, where one player covered the top of the key, three others stretched in a line across the middle, and the last protected the baseline. The one-two-two setup found two players covering the middle and two at the baseline while the last stuck to the ball carrier. Then there was Julian's favorite, the two-one-two. That's when two players hovered near the top corners of the key and two took the back corners while the team's fifth player — usually Julian or Cal — caused problems for the opposing offense by dancing around in the middle with their long arms stretched high and wide.

Before the game, the coach had instructed the Tornadoes to use two-one-two. Julian backpedaled the last few steps into the center of the key, keeping an eye on the ball carrier at all times. It was a good thing he did, too, because the nimble guard darted forward and tossed up a running jumper!

If Julian had still had his back to the Jet, the shot might have gone in. But he saw the shot coming, leaped, and *slap!* smacked the ball away with the flat of his hand.

It bounced once before Len grabbed it. By that time, Mick was halfway down the court. He lifted a hand in the air, looking for a quick pass.

Unfortunately, Len tripped over his own feet before he set the fast break in motion. He fell with a thud. The ball bounced over the sideline.

Tweet!

"Jets!" the referee cried.

Len picked himself up, looking embarrassed. The ref scooped up the ball and handed it to a Jet guard. The guard inbounded it to the tall center. The center almost bobbled the catch. When he did control the ball, he took a few awkward dribbles and then passed it back very quickly.

Interesting, Julian thought as he watched the exchange. *The center has trouble handling the ball. Maybe there's a way to make that work for us!*

10

3

Julian didn't mention his observation to the coach right away. Instead, he kept a careful eye on the Jet center as the first quarter continued.

During those minutes, the mustached player rarely dribbled or passed. His primary role seemed to be that of shooter and rebounder. Time and again, his teammates worked the ball around the key and then fed it to him to shoot. Sometimes his shots went in. But just as often, they clanged off the rim or rebounded with great force off the backboard.

Guess being tall and hairy isn't everything, Julian thought gleefully as yet another of the center's jumpers misfired.

The quarter ended with the Tornadoes up, 12 points to 8. It was a nice lead, and one to which Julian had contributed five points. But Julian thought he knew how they could make that point gap much

11

bigger. So when the buzzer sounded, he hurried to the bench to talk to the coach.

"Coach, I've been watching their center and —"

"And you've noted that he's got great height, but not great ballhandling skills, right?" the coach said with a smile.

"Exactly! Do you think we should turn up the pressure on him? If we double-teamed him whenever he gets the ball, I bet he'd start to miss *all* his shots instead of just some of them!"

Coach Valenti pursed his lips in thought. "I hear what you're saying, Julian. But let's hold off on that for now. After all, we're winning without having to change our game plan. If he becomes a scoring threat, perhaps then we'll tighten up our grip on him."

Julian was about to protest when the coach added, "Put the shoe on the other foot, Julian. How would you feel if the Jets coach decided to target *you* that way, when the point advantage was already on their side?" He shook his head. "In my book, that's not sportsmanlike."

Julian blinked. Then he nodded slowly. "Okay, coach. I get what you're saying."

Coach Valenti patted him on the back. "You're going to be a valuable asset to your new team."

Grady, who was walking by just then, stopped and stared.

"New team? What new team, Julian?"

By then, several other players were listening. Julian shifted uncomfortably. "Yeah, um, I guess I forgot to tell you guys. Coach Valenti pulled a few strings and got me on a team in my new town. It's called the Warriors. My folks thought it'd be a good way for me to meet kids."

"And make new friends," Grady mumbled.

Julian scuffed his sneaker on the shiny wood floor and shrugged. "I suppose. But that doesn't mean we still won't be friends, right? I'm only moving an hour and a half away, after all!"

Grady looked up at him from under his floppy hair. To Julian's relief, he smiled.

"Course we're still going to be friends! That's why texting was invented." He held up his hands and waggled his thumbs. "And you're looking at the fastest texter in the county, buddy-boy!" He blew on his thumbs as if they were smoking hot.

Everyone was laughing so loudly that the referee had to whistle twice before they heard him. Julian and Grady jogged onto the court for the second quarter, slapping palms as they parted to go to their positions.

13

I'm really gonna miss him, Julian thought. Then the whistle blew again and the game resumed.

The Tornadoes had possession, so Grady took the ball out-of-bounds. At the referee's signal, he passed the ball in to Len, who sent it back once Grady stepped over the sideline.

Grady dribbled past the half-court line. Suddenly, two Jet players rushed forward, wedging him into a tight double-team. Their hands flashed forward as they each attempted to steal the ball. Julian saw a panicked look cross Grady's face. He willed his friend to dribble his way out of the clutch. But Grady didn't. He grabbed the ball and held it.

Now Grady was stuck. He couldn't put the ball to the floor again because he'd be called for double-dribble. He needed help — fast! Julian started forward only to see Mick dash toward the sideline, waving for Grady to pass. Grady lifted the ball high.

Julian groaned inwardly. Grady was practically telling the opposition that he was about to do an over-head pass!

Sure enough, the defense rose up out of their crouches and raised their arms high. But the steal Julian thought was about to come never happened.

No sooner had the defense straightened up tall than Grady bent down and laced a neat bounce pass between them, right into Mick's waiting hands!

"Yes!" Julian cheered along with his teammates and their fans. "Beautiful!"

Grady didn't waste time acknowledging the applause. He raced around the dumbfounded defenders and received the return pass from Mick. He held up two fingers and then one finger with his free hand.

He wasn't flashing the peace sign or pointing to the ceiling. He was telling his teammates which play he wanted to run.

The play was known as "two-one," for two passes and one fake. It was fairly simple. But it would only work if the three players involved made rapid-fire, accurate passes.

Grady started it off by zipping the ball to Len on his right. Len quickly bounced it to Julian. Those were the two passes. Now Julian faked a jump shot aimed at drawing the defense to him. Sure enough, two Jets jumped out in front of him, leaving the door to the basket wide open. At the same time, Len cut to the hoop.

Julian and Len had practiced the next move over and over. That practice paid off now. Len glanced back. Julian hit him with a clean, chest-high pass. Len caught the ball in front of the hoop, took one more step, and launched off the ground for a reverse layup.

Bam! Swish! The ball struck the backboard at just the right angle. The white strings danced as the orange sphere dropped through the net.

Len pumped his fist and pointed a finger at Julian. Julian flashed him a smile and single thumbs-up.

Man, he thought gleefully, *I love it when a play works like it's supposed to!*

4

The plays continued to work well for the remainder of the first half. When the buzzer sounded for the break, the score stood at Tornadoes 20, Jets 12.

Coach Valenti clapped his hands. "Good playing out there, boys. Now you five take a rest and we'll give some other Tornadoes a chance to show what they can do. Cal, you go in at center. Roger and Warren, go in for Mick and Terrell at forward. Brandon and Anthony will be our guards. Anthony, we have possession so you inbound the ball."

Julian hated being taken out of games. But he understood — and agreed with — the league rule that stated all players must be given court time every game. After all, players who rode the bench would never improve. They would never feel like members of the team, either, unless they took an active part in each win and every loss.

Still, watching the action from the sidelines wasn't nearly as much fun as being in the thick of it!

As it turned out, however, he didn't get back into the thick of it that quarter. The Jets struggled against the substitutes just as they had against the starters. When the buzzer sounded, ending the third quarter, the score had jumped from 20–12 to 28–18 in favor of the Tornadoes!

The mood on the Tornadoes' bench was upbeat. Coach Valenti praised them for their efforts but also reminded them that they still had a quarter yet to play. "Bring the same energy to the court for the last minutes and you'll do great!"

Julian and the others shouted in unison. Then Julian hurried to the fountain to refill his water bottle. As he did, Cal appeared at his side.

"Julian, I was wondering, after the game . . . could you give me some advice on how to play center? You know, since it looks like I'll be in the starting slot after today."

Julian blinked. Until that moment, he hadn't thought about Cal taking the opening tip-off and running plays like the two-one in his place. A sudden surge of jealousy coursed through him.

But it disappeared just as quickly as it came. After all, Cal worked hard. He deserved his shot at starting center — in fact, if Julian hadn't been on the team, chances were Cal would already be the starter.

"You don't need any advice from me," Julian said. "You're doing great out there! You've scored what, seven points already this game? Heck, I should be asking you for pointers!"

But when he tried to walk past Cal, the other boy moved in front of him. "No, seriously, I, uh, I'd really like to hear your thoughts on playing center."

Julian frowned in puzzlement. "I don't have any thoughts, Cal. I just practice the plays so I'm ready to use them in games."

"Practice the plays, huh? Interesting." Cal nodded vigorously. "Tell me more!"

"Tell you more?" Now Julian was totally confused. "There's nothing to tell! After all, you do the same plays I do every practice. You take the same shots. You — Hello? Cal? Are you even listening to me?"

Cal had been looking intently at Julian. But all of a sudden, his gaze shifted to a spot over Julian's left shoulder. He gave a slight nod.

"What are you looking at?" Julian asked, turning

around. Behind him, Coach Valenti, Grady, Len, and several other players were huddled together. He looked back at Cal. "What's going on?"

Cal widened his eyes, giving him a look of innocence. "What makes you think something's going on? Unless you mean the game? Yep, seems like that's about to go on in a sec! Come on!"

Cal pushed past Julian to join the others. After a moment, Julian followed. He was certain Cal's nod had been in reply to some signal. But what? Who had given it? And why? There was no time to ask any of those questions, however, because he and the other starters had to get on the floor.

The Jets had possession. Their stocky point guard took the ball out-of-bounds at the mid-court line and waited for the referee's whistle.

Tweet!

The guard bounced the ball to a teammate and then took the return pass. He dribbled carefully toward the key. His eyes darted to and fro as he searched for an open man.

Suddenly, he stopped and slapped the ball. An instant later, the tall Jets center took an angled step backward toward the baseline. Julian mirrored him, certain his man was trying to squeeze around him.

He was wrong! That step was a fake — and it had worked perfectly! Julian whirled around in time to see the center dash into the key, nab a high-flying pass, and lay the ball into the net for two points.

Julian trotted down the court, shaking his head at his mistake. Then he grinned inwardly. *Since this is a game of "last times,"* he thought, *guess I'll just have that be the last time I fall for that stagger-step!*

He didn't get faked out again that way, but there were other moments in the game where the Jets fooled him, and other Tornadoes, too. Still, their opponents' efforts weren't enough to push them ahead of the Tornadoes. When the game ended, the final score was Tornadoes 42, Jets 29.

Julian joined his teammates for the traditional hand-slap, good-game exchange with the Jets. Then he turned to go back to the bench. But he'd only gone a single step when Coach Valenti barked out his name.

"Julian Pryce! Where do you think you're going? I don't remember telling you to leave the court!"

5

Julian was startled by the stern tone in his coach's voice. "I'm sorry, sir," he started to stammer. But the words died on his lips when he turned around to face the coach.

Because it wasn't just the coach standing there, it was the entire Tornado team! Coach Valenti and Cal held a banner emblazoned with the words "GOOD LUCK, JULIAN! WE'LL MISS YOU!"

Grady was holding something too — a basketball, Julian saw. Then he looked closer and realized there was writing all over the ball.

"We all signed it," Grady said. "That way, you'll always remember who was on the best basketball team in the world."

Julian took the ball and turned it slowly in his hands, reading the signatures. He swallowed hard. "Gosh, I don't know what to say," he murmured.

Then something struck him. He looked up. "Hang on. You guys didn't know I was leaving until before the game. When did you do this?"

Cal gave him a sheepish look. "You know when I was asking you all those questions before the last quarter?"

Julian started laughing. "You were keeping me from seeing everyone sign it! Man, and I just thought you were getting all weird on me!"

The other boys laughed along with him. Then Julian thanked them all again for the ball and shook hands with the coach. "It's been awesome playing for you, Coach Valenti. I hope . . ."

He was about to say that he hoped his new coach would be as good. But his throat suddenly had a lump in it that the words couldn't get past.

The coach put a hand on Julian's shoulder and said, "Any coach would be lucky to have you on his team."

"Thank you, sir." Julian balanced his autographed basketball on his fingertip and gave it a brisk spin. "For everything."

Julian's parents and sister appeared on the court just then.

"Good game, son," Mr. Pryce said.

"Yeah, except for that time the tall kid caught you

with your pants down, you looked pretty decent," Megan added with a grin.

"Ha, ha," Julian said, making a face at her.

"You must be hungry after all that running around," Mrs. Pryce said. She looked around at the other players. "You all must be hungry. What do you say we head to Cutler's Candy and Ice Cream Emporium for a victory celebration?"

"Really?" Julian loved Cutler's, but was surprised to hear his mother offer to take them there. She wasn't big on giving her kids lots of sweets.

"Sure. It's our treat," she said. "Go see who can join us, okay?"

Julian quickly made the rounds through the team. Everybody said they could go, so ten minutes later, the whole team showed up at the Emporium. When the owner, Mrs. Cutler, saw them, she opened a special party room at the back of the store and ushered them in.

"That way, you can eat your ice cream and treats together," she said. "Now come on up to the counter and tell me what you'd like."

Choosing a treat was difficult for Julian. He loved Cutler's peppermint ice cream, especially when it was covered with hot fudge and whipped cream, and topped with a cherry. But he also loved Cutler's famous Triple Chocolate Peanut Butter Drops — small balls of creamy peanut butter surrounded by layers of milk, white, and dark chocolate.

In the end, he chose the ice cream because that's what everyone else was getting.

"I don't suppose you deliver your candy, do you, Mrs. Cutler?" he asked, only half-joking. "Because I'm moving on Saturday and I don't know when I'll get your Triple Chocolate Peanut Butter Drops again!"

With a smile, she reached into the display case and took out three drops. "These are on the house. Call 'em a good-bye present."

Julian smiled and thanked her before popping one of the drops into his mouth.

"Good?" Mrs. Cutler inquired with raised eyebrows.

"Fantastic," Julian said through a delicious mouthful of peanut butter and chocolate. "Thanks again!"

Mrs. Cutler nodded. Then she left to help another customer.

Julian headed into the back room and slid into a space next to Mick. "Hey, bro, what'd you get?" he asked. "I got a hot fudge sundae with peppermint ice cream."

Mick sniffed the air, a confused look on his face. "Weird. Your peppermint smells a lot like peanut butter!"

Julian laughed and explained where the peanut butter smell was coming from. "She gave me three for free. Want one?" He held out a drop.

Mick waved it away. "Nah, I can get them any time. Thanks, though."

Julian was about to eat the drop himself when a hand swooped in and snatched it away.

"Hey!" He spun around just in time to see Grady toss the candy into the air and catch it in his mouth.

"Mmmm, thanks!" the other boy said.

Julian jumped up and grabbed Grady in a choke hold from behind. "I'll teach you to steal my candy!" he cried as he rubbed his knuckles though Grady's hair.

"Okay! Okay! You want it back? Here!" Grady stuck out his tongue, showing everybody at the table the chocolate-peanut butter sludge on it.

"Gross!"

"Ewww!"

"Aw, man, you just ruined my appetite!"

The mock-disgusted shouts mixed in with Grady's laughter. He laughed even harder when Julian started knuckling his hair again.

Then suddenly a new voice joined the chatter.

"Are you guys fighting again?"

Julian and Grady froze. Then as one, they cried, "Barry!"

Julian let go of Grady and hurried to his friend's side. Barry was leaning on his crutches. His right leg was encased in a thick cast that had once been white but had turned a dull gray in the weeks he'd had it on. His left arm was wrapped in an Ace bandage. His face still bore yellowish bruises and scars from the auto accident.

"What are you doing here?" Julian asked as he helped Barry to a seat.

"Gee, thanks, nice to see you, too," Barry replied sarcastically.

"You know what I mean!"

Barry grinned. "Yeah, I know. Your mom called my mom a few minutes ago." He nodded toward the door, where Mrs. Pryce was talking with Mrs. Streeter. Then he narrowed his eyes and added, "Your mom's been calling my mom a lot lately, actually. At first I figured she wanted to know how I was doing. Turns out, she was asking my mom for advice about selling your house!"

Julian's face turned hot with embarrassment. "Um, yeah, I meant to tell you —"

"— that you're moving on Saturday?" Barry cut in. "So I hear. But not from you!"

"I'm sorry, Barry. I should have told you," Julian admitted. "But I've been sort of denying it myself, I guess. Moving away wasn't my idea, after all!"

"Really?" Barry said. "It was such a lousy idea, I figured it *had* to be yours!"

Julian aimed a swing at Barry's head. Barry ducked, laughing, and then called out, "Which one of you is going to get me some ice cream?"

"I'll get it," Grady said, hopping to his feet.

"Thanks. I'll have —"

"— a double scoop of lemon sherbet with hot caramel and whipped cream," Julian and Grady said together.

"How'd you know?" Barry asked.

Grady rolled his eyes. "You get the same disgusting combination every time," he said. "Be right back."

Be right back. See you in a few. I'll be over soon. As of Saturday, Julian would no longer be saying any of those things to anyone here. Because he'd be moving away that day, to a town where he knew exactly no one.

28

6

The next three days were a flurry of activity for Julian. On Thursday, he cleaned out his desk and his locker and said good-bye to all his teachers and classmates. He didn't go to school on Friday. Instead, he and his sister stayed home to help their mother pack up the last of their belongings.

"It's weird being home when everyone else is in school," Megan said as she taped up a box of books in the living room.

"Yeah, I feel like I should have a fever or something," Julian agreed. He reached for a stack of CDs.

Megan glanced at their mother, who was talking on the phone, and then leaned toward Julian. "I don't know about you," she said in a low voice, "but I feel sick when I imagine walking into the new school our first day."

Julian knew exactly what she meant. Every time

29

he thought about being the new kid, his stomach somersaulted like an Olympic gymnast going for a gold medal.

Mrs. Pryce hung up the phone. "So," she said brightly, "how are things going? Need any more packing supplies?"

"No," both Julian and Megan replied.

"Okay, then!" Mrs. Pryce bent down to pick up the box of books Megan had just taped shut. But when she lifted it, the bottom flaps tore open. Books rained down on the floor below.

"Oh, no!" Megan cried. "I'm sorry, Mom! I guess I packed it too full." She hurried over to clean up the mess.

Mrs. Pryce didn't move. She just stood there, holding the broken box. Then finally she shook her head. "It's okay, Megan, just leave it for now. Come on, you two, let's go to the kitchen and have a snack and a chat."

Julian and Megan followed their mother into the kitchen. Much of that room had already been packed, but Mrs. Pryce found a stack of paper plates and some cups. She put cookies on one plate and filled three cups with lemonade. That was the snack — but the chat didn't come as quickly. Instead, the only sounds in the kitchen were the crunch of cookie and the slurp of lemonade.

Finally, Mrs. Pryce said, "I know this move is tough on you guys. Believe me, if there was any way we could stay here, we would. But we can't. Dad's new job is just too far away. If we didn't move, he'd be on the road for more than three hours each day. And that's three hours he wouldn't have to spend with us."

Julian was about to say that he understood when there was a knock on the door. "I'll get it," he said.

When he opened the door he was surprised to find Barry and Mrs. Streeter on the other side. He stepped aside to let them in. "What're you doing here?" he asked Barry. "School doesn't get out for another two hours!"

"I had a doctor's appointment after lunch," Barry replied. "I convinced Mom to bring me here instead of back to school." He grinned. "Getting my way has been the only good thing about this accident!"

"I heard that!" Mrs. Streeter called.

"Come on, let's go to my room," Julian said. Then he looked at Barry's crutches. "If you think you can handle the stairs, that is."

"No sweat," Barry said confidently. "How do you think I get to my own room every night?"

"I hadn't thought of that," Julian admitted.

"Yeah, that's you all over — thoughtless!"

"Ha, ha," Julian said. "At least let me take your backpack."

"Nah, I can handle it." As if to prove his point, Barry swung forward on his crutches, making his way out of the kitchen and into the living room where he maneuvered deftly through the boxes and around the spilled books. Then he hopped up the stairs.

"At least your room hasn't changed," Barry said as he flopped down onto Julian's bed. "Still filled with mementos from last season, huh?" His voice sounded wistful.

"And one thing from this season, too," Julian said, pointing to the autographed basketball. Then he took a framed photograph of the previous year's Tornadoes team from the wall and handed it to Barry. "There we all are, in our glory!"

Barry studied the photo for a moment and then put it aside. "You ever hear from Max? Or Art or Danny?"

Julian shook his head. "Do you?"

"Max, no. I see Art and Danny sometimes. But now that they're in high school, well, you know . . ." He shrugged. "I sure hope you're better at staying in touch than they are."

Julian smiled. "You'll be hearing from me so often, it'll be like I'm still here!"

Barry gave a little laugh. "If only!"

They were silent for a moment. Then Barry removed his backpack and opened it. "Got something for you," he said. He pulled out a wrapped box and handed it to Julian.

"What is it?" Julian asked.

"Uh, duh, you're supposed to open it and find out!"

Julian tore off the paper and threw it at Barry. Then he looked at the box. *Cutler's* was stamped in huge chocolate brown letters across the top. A huge grin split Julian's face. "You didn't!"

Barry waggled his eyebrows. "Mick, Grady, and I pooled our money to get them for you."

Julian lifted the box's lid. Inside were at least a hundred Triple Chocolate Peanut Butter Drops!

"Awesome!"

He reached in to take one. Barry slapped his hand away.

"Don't eat them now!"

"Why not?"

"You're supposed to save them until you get to your new house. Then, every time you eat some, you'll

33

think of us. And when you do, you'll pick up the phone and call. Or grab your cell and text. Or turn on your computer and e-mail. Or pick up a pen and write!"

"Or send a carrier pigeon with a message tied to its leg! Or build a fire and make smoke signals!" Julian said, laughing.

"Morse code! Pony express! Semaphore flags! The options are endless!" Barry cried.

"Okay, I get it!" Julian said. "I'll stay in touch, I promise! But you have to stay in touch with me too!"

Barry flopped back on the bed and waved his hand dismissively. "Me? No way, man. I'll be too busy."

Barry and his mother stayed for the rest of the afternoon and helped the Pryces pack. They stayed for pizza, too, and then said their final good-byes.

The house seemed much emptier after they left. Julian went to his room, laid on his bed, and stared at his empty walls.

"It's really happening," he murmured. "We're leaving tomorrow. And we're not coming back."

7

Four days later, Julian walked down a long hallway behind his new school's principal. Mrs. Oliver's high heels rang out loudly against the tile. One of Julian's sneakers squeaked with every other step. Together, they sounded like an off-beat percussion section in a band — clack-clack-squeak, clack-clack-squeak.

Then they reached Julian's new classroom and the rhythm stopped. "Here we are, Julian." Mrs. Oliver swept open the door and stepped aside so he could walk in.

Julian had promised himself that he wouldn't be nervous. But the moment he entered the room, his heart began to hammer in his chest. There were only twenty-one kids in the class, but it seemed like hundreds!

"Ms. Pierce, this is the boy I was telling you about,"

Mrs. Oliver said. "Julian Pryce, this is Ms. Pierce, your teacher."

Ms. Pierce looked as sharp as her name — needlenosed, with bony arms and long, skinny fingers. But when she spoke, her voice was soft and soothing. "Good morning, Julian," she said. "Welcome to my class."

Mrs. Oliver nodded and left. Julian stood awkwardly, unsure of what he should do next. To his relief, Ms. Pierce came to his rescue.

"Take that empty desk," she said, pointing toward a seat near the windows, "and stow your gear on the floor. I'll find you a locker later."

Julian did as instructed. Then came the request he'd been dreading.

"Why don't you tell us a little bit about yourself?" Ms. Pierce suggested.

Twenty-one pairs of eyes turned to look at him.

Julian shifted in his seat. "Um, well, my name's Julian. But I guess you know that already."

He heard a few titters from the back of the class. Ms. Pierce frowned and the sound stopped.

"I'm thirteen," Julian continued. "We moved here because my dad got a new job."

He paused, unsure of what to say next.

"Do you have any hobbies, or play any sports?" Ms. Pierce prodded.

"I play basketball. I was my team's starting center. We were called the Tornadoes. Maybe you heard of us? We went undefeated last year."

He looked around hopefully. Nobody responded. "Well, anyway, we were looking good this year too." Thinking of his old team made Julian's throat close up. He stopped talking.

A tall boy in the back of the class cleared his throat. "You plan to play here?"

"I'll be playing on a team called the Warriors."

"Then you should know something." The boy leaned forward, narrowed his eyes, and jabbed a finger at his chest. "*I'm* the starting center for the Warriors."

"*Paul*," Ms. Pierce admonished. "Please."

Paul sat back but didn't take his eyes off of Julian. Julian looked away.

Great, he thought. *I've been here for all of five minutes and already I've made an enemy. And wouldn't you know it's a guy on my new team!*

He made a silent vow to steer clear of Paul if he could. And he made good on that vow for the rest of the day — a day that passed in a blur of changing classes, finding his locker and forgetting his lock combination, and sitting by himself during lunch. He'd never been happier to hear the final bell ring.

Mrs. Pryce picked him and Megan up after school. Megan chatted gaily about the new friends she had made. Mrs. Pryce told them that she'd made good progress in unpacking more of their belongings.

Julian barely listened. He was too busy worrying about what was to happen one hour from now: his first practice with the Warriors.

So much for avoiding Paul, he thought.

When he got home, he had a quick snack and changed into his basketball clothes. Then he set off for the town's community center. The center had a basketball court, weight rooms, batting cages, and an Olympic-size pool. The complex was only a few blocks from his house. Still, Julian walked briskly. He didn't want to be late and give Paul reason to come down on him.

Another team was just finishing its turn on the court when he arrived. Julian sat down to watch them.

They were high school players by the looks of them. One player in particular caught Julian's eye, for two reasons. First, he looked so much like Paul that at first, Julian thought it *was* Paul. But then he heard another player call him Peter, so he decided the two must be related, perhaps even brothers.

And the second reason Peter stood out was because he was the best dribbler Julian had ever seen. Behind the back, through the legs, around defenders with a single head fake, all the way down the court with three guys chasing him — Peter could do it all!

"I wish Grady could take lessons from him!"

"Who's Grady?"

Julian started. He hadn't realized he'd spoken the words out loud. Nor had he seen or heard the boy slide into the bleacher behind him. Now he turned to look at him.

The boy grinned. "Hi. I'm Alex Harrison. Who are you?"

Julian told him his name.

Alex's grin broadened. "You're the new kid, right?"

Julian nodded.

"Thought so. Let's see. You led your league in rebounds and scoring two years ago and came in second in assists. Your team, the Tornadoes, went undefeated. So far this year, you've scored at least twelve points every game you played. Three wins and two losses, if I'm not wrong."

Julian raised his eyebrows. "How'd you know all that?"

Alex laughed. "You can find out all kinds of stuff on the Internet. I just typed your name into the search line and *ta-da*! A whole ton of information popped up."

Julian smiled. "So have you ever typed your own name in?"

Alex made a face. "Once. All that popped up was a big bag of empty. Guess I haven't really done anything Web-worthy!"

"Oh." Julian didn't know what to say to that so he changed the subject. "So you play for the Warriors too?"

"I wear the uniform, but play? Not so much. Mostly I ride the pine while the starters run the court."

"You must see some playing time," Julian protested. He was thinking about his old league's rule where everyone got into every game.

Alex shrugged. "A minute here, a minute there. But Coach Boyd likes to win, so . . ." He shrugged again.

Julian wanted to ask more, but at that moment Coach Boyd himself strode into the gym. The coach was a powerfully built man with a buzz cut. Even though he was indoors, he wore sunglasses. He surveyed the gym, spotted the boys, and walked unhurriedly toward them.

"Hello, Harrison," he said. He studied Julian for a moment. "You must be Pryce."

Julian scrambled to his feet. Coach Boyd was such a commanding presence that he had to restrain himself to keep from saluting. "Yes sir," he said. "I'm Julian Pryce."

Coach Boyd nodded once. "Show him to the locker room, Harrison. Report back in five minutes."

Julian glanced at the clock. "Doesn't practice start in fifteen minutes?" He thought maybe he'd gotten the time wrong.

Coach Boyd slowly removed his sunglasses. "It does," he said. His voice was mild. But the look he leveled at Julian was so stern that Julian shrank back. "I'd like to see you in action before the others get here. *If* that's okay with you?"

Julian gulped. "I —"

"Of course, sir," Alex cut in. "We'll be right back." He grabbed Julian by the arm and tugged him toward the locker room.

8

The door closed behind the boys with a gentle click. Only then did Julian let out the breath he'd been holding. "Is he always like that?"

Alex laughed. "You mean unbelievably scary and with no sense of humor at all? Yeah. He is."

"Oh."

"I take it your old coach wasn't the same way?"

Julian snorted. "Not at all! He was tough and he kept us in line. But he was fair and, well, a good guy."

He sank down on the nearest bench. He'd known he would miss his teammates. But he hadn't suspected he'd miss Coach Valenti just as much!

Alex sat next to him. "Aw, you'll get used to him. He's not that bad, so long as you follow his rules and do what he says, when he says it, and exactly how he tells you to do it, no questions asked!"

"Great." Then Julian looked up. "You asked earlier

who Grady was. He was a guard on my old team." *And one of my best friends*, he added to himself. He wondered if Alex might be a friend too, and if he and Grady might meet one day. He hoped so. He liked Alex.

"That's why you noticed Peter — otherwise known as the future of the National Basketball Association?" Alex said now.

Julian's eyes widened. "Really? He's going into the NBA?"

Alex cracked up. "Well, he thinks he is, and Coach Boyd thinks he is. But so far, the NBA doesn't seem aware of it!"

Julian was confused. "Why does Coach Boyd care what Peter does?"

Alex sobered up. "Peter's last name is Boyd. He's the coach's son."

"Does Peter have a brother named Paul?" Julian asked.

Alex rolled his eyes. "You met him, huh? Yeah, he's our starting center. He can be a good guy, but sometimes his ego is out of control."

Julian thought of the overly confident way Paul had announced that he was the starting center of the Warriors. "I can only imagine," he said.

Alex stood. "Time's up," he said regretfully. "Ready to show the coach what you can do?"

"As ready as I'll ever be." But for the first time in a long time, Julian wasn't sure he *was* ready.

The high school squad was clearing the court when Julian and Alex emerged. Coach Boyd was in deep discussion with the high school coach. The two boys stood at a distance, waiting for him to finish.

"You've got to give him more opportunities to shoot," Julian overheard Coach Boyd say. "If he doesn't rack up the stats this year, the NBA scouts will overlook him!"

The other coach held up his hands as if to fend off an attack. "With all due respect, Boyd, your boy's shot isn't good enough for me to design plays around. If he'd just practice more . . ."

Coach Boyd bristled. "He practices plenty! What he needs is the chance to shoot during *game* situations! Now are you going to give him those chances or not?"

Just then, the high school coach caught Julian and Alex listening. "We'll finish this conversation another time," he said curtly. "Your players are waiting for you."

Coach Boyd started to protest. But the other coach walked away before he could get another word out. Coach Boyd spun around and almost ran into Julian.

"Who —? Oh, right. Pryce." He cleared his throat and pointed to the court. "Grab a basketball and take some jump shots from different places on the floor. Harrison, rebound for him."

Julian and Alex hurried onto the floor. Julian dribbled to the right corner of the key, and then lofted the ball in a gentle arc toward the hoop. It banked in, swishing the net strings as it passed through.

Alex nabbed the ball and fed it back to Julian. Julian shot from the left corner of the key this time. Again he made the basket and again, Alex returned the ball to him.

He and Alex got into a rhythm. Now, instead of waiting for Alex to pass and then dribbling to a new spot, Julian shot, ran to another position, and looked for the pass. Alex hit him cleanly every time. Julian sank many of his shots, but he missed a few too. One miss clanged off the rim with such force that it bounced high over his head — and into Paul Boyd's hands.

Paul tucked the ball under his arm. "Guess I don't have to worry about the new guy taking my slot, do I?" he said in a loud, mocking voice. "Here you go, Pryce." He handed over the ball with exaggerated care.

Julian glowered, but held his tongue. *I won't let him*

45

get to me, he told himself. Then he bit back a smile. *I know what I'll do!* I'll *get to* him *instead — by out-playing him! Sitting on the bench while I rule the court should teach him a lesson!*

Coach Boyd took command of the practice then. He introduced Julian with a blunt, "This is Pryce." He didn't bother to tell Julian who any of his new teammates were.

When Julian played for the Tornadoes, Coach Valenti had started practices with simple drills designed to warm up his players.

But Coach Boyd did things differently. He divided the players into two squads. He sent Julian's group to one basket with instructions to shoot, pass, dribble, and rebound. He ushered the other group to the opposite basket.

Alex was in Julian's group. He took a few moments to point out the other Warriors. "This redheaded doofus is Riley," he said, earning a whap on the head from Riley. "That's Skeeter over there with the headband. Riley and Skeeter play guard. Steve-o is the one with the short black hair. He and Chip — the guy with the fake tattoos on his arm — are forwards. I play forward, too, by the way." He made a face. "At least I think those are our positions. It's hard to tell when you don't see much playing time, right, guys?"

The other Warriors murmured their agreement.

Julian tried to hide his surprise. None of them played regularly? If that was true, and he was there with them, it could only mean one thing: He'd be sitting on the bench too!

He glanced at the other end of the court. Coach Boyd was huddled with five Warriors — the starting lineup, Julian suddenly realized. His heart squeezed.

That's where I should be, he thought. *I'm a good player! He just doesn't know it yet.*

But the question was, how would he show Coach Boyd what he could do if the coach never even looked his way?

9

Hey, Pryce, heads up!"

Julian snapped out of his daze in time to catch Steve-o's bounce pass. He hesitated for a moment and then swept the ball up and over his shoulder and into the hoop with a neat hook shot.

Steve-o whistled in appreciation. "Not bad, Pryce!" he said.

Julian caught the ball before it hit the floor and shrugged. "Thanks. And if you don't mind, could you call me Julian?"

"Why would I call you that?"

"Because it's my name! Pryce is my last name."

Steve-o started laughing. "Oh! Sorry! I thought — never mind. Show me that hook shot again, will you?"

Julian did. This time the ball rolled around the rim twice and then fell outside the rim. Julian's face turned hot.

"So, um, I guess we should get going on a drill or something, right?" he said to cover his embarrassment.

Riley sank a lazy jump shot. "Why?"

Julian blinked. "Won't Coach Boyd get mad if he sees us standing around doing nothing?"

Riley and Steve-o looked at each other and then back at Julian. "He'll be too busy with the starters to notice," Riley said at last. He took another shot. It fell through the net without even touching the rim.

"So what are we supposed to do?" Julian asked incredulously. "Coach ourselves for the next hour?"

Chip dribbled past him and put in a soft layup. "Pretty much, yeah. Unless you've got a better idea?"

Julian thumped the ball down in a hard dribble. "Yeah, I got a better idea! Let's run some drills or something! Work on improving our skills!"

"What kind of drill?" Alex wanted to know.

Julian thought back to the drills Coach Valenti had run. "How about the three-man weave?"

His suggestion was met with blank stares.

"Don't you guys know the weave?" Julian asked. "It's simple. Three guys line up together. The guy in the middle has the ball. He passes to the player on his right and then runs behind him. That player dribbles a

49

few steps to the middle, passes to the guy on the left, and then runs behind *him*. And so on, down the court, dribbling, passing, trading places, until one of the players reaches a spot close enough to the basket to shoot. You've never done it before?"

Chip nodded. "I remember doing it, actually. But that was a few years ago, when I was playing on another team. I liked that drill. Let's do it!"

The boys divided into two groups of three and moved toward center court. Julian saw Coach Boyd look toward them and frown. But he didn't interfere.

Julian, Riley, and Alex were in the first group. Julian had the ball in the middle. He passed to Riley, saying, "Dribble toward my spot!"

Riley did so.

"Alex, you come forward a few steps to meet him! Riley, pass to Alex!" Julian called.

Alex hurried to catch Riley's pass. Unfortunately, Riley forgot he was supposed to run behind Alex and the two boys nearly collided.

"That's okay, just keep going!" Julian said, slowing his pace so he was still in line with the other two. "You'll get the hang of it after a few times through."

They did get the hang of it, although the drill wasn't anywhere near as smooth as it had been when Julian did it with the Tornadoes. Still, it was better than standing around shooting aimlessly, he thought.

His new teammates seemed to think so too. After fifteen minutes, they were sweating, breathing hard, and grinning with enthusiasm.

"You know, I remember another drill I used to do," Chip said between gasps. "We line up in pairs facing each other. Each pair has a ball. We shuffle sideways down the court, passing back and forth."

"Bounce pass or chest pass?" Skeeter cut in.

"Both," Chip replied. "Mix it up. When a pair gets to the end, the person with the ball shoots. The other one rebounds. Then they peel off and head to center court to begin again."

Julian nodded. "Let's do it."

They paired off and began. Julian had often run a sideways shuffle drill with the Tornadoes, but without the ball. Instead, Coach Valenti had had them crouch as low as they could and shuffle crab-like, all around the lines on the court. Julian hadn't been fond of the drill, but now he realized how helpful it had been. His legs were stronger for it and so, unlike his teammates, he had no trouble staying low.

They did the passing drill for several minutes. Then Julian suggested they try a two-against-one defense drill. He volunteered to be the first man to play defense.

Alex and Skeeter came at him, dribbling and passing. Julian hovered near the top of the key, biding his time. Then Skeeter drew near to him with the ball — and Julian pounced.

"Yikes!" Skeeter stopped his dribble — and groaned when he realized he was stuck. He didn't have a clear shot because Julian was between him and the basket, waving his arms high. So he tried to pass to Alex, only to have Julian drop his arms and snatch the ball away.

"Man, you're quick for a big guy!" Skeeter said.

"Thanks. You guys might have gotten around me, though, if Alex had come forward for that pass."

"Or if I hadn't panicked and stopped dribbling," Skeeter admonished himself. "Then we could have done a pick-and-roll."

Julian nodded. "Always a good move in a two-on-one situation. If Alex had planted himself just behind me, you could have taken off to the hoop. When I turned to follow you, I would have run right into him!"

"Right *through* me is more like it," Alex said, laughing. "You outweigh me by at least fifteen pounds!" He stood right next to Julian and stuck out a leg. "And I bet your legs are five inches taller than mine."

"Well, you know what they say: 'the taller they are, the harder they fall,'" Julian quipped.

The words were barely out of his mouth when Coach Boyd suddenly appeared at his side. "What's going on here?" he barked.

"I — we were just doing a defense drill, sir," Julian stammered.

"I'm well aware of what you were doing, Pryce," Coach Boyd interrupted. "I see everything that happens on my court. Understand?"

A movement beyond the coach's shoulder caught Julian's eye. It was Paul, nudging a teammate and laughing silently at Julian.

"I asked you a question, Pryce!" Coach Boyd barked.

"Yes sir," Julian replied. "I understand." *But I doubt you really do see everything that happens,* he added silently. *If you did, you'd see that you're wasting talented players — and spending too much time with your jerk of a son!*

10

Coach Boyd instructed Julian and the others subs to join the rest of the team. Julian caught Alex's eye as they hurried down the court. He wanted to ask the other boy why the coach was so angry. But Alex shook his head as if to warn Julian not to speak, so Julian kept his mouth shut.

"All right," Coach Boyd said when they were gathered together. "Chip, Skeeter, Steve-o, Riley, and Alex, get on the court. You'll be going man-to-man against the starters."

"What should I do?" Julian asked.

"Sit on the bench," the coach said without looking at him. "And watch and learn."

Paul and the four other starters — Julian realized with a jolt that he didn't even know their names — readied themselves at the center court line. Paul caught the ball from his father. He thumped it twice

54

against his palm and then started to dribble. The starters moved with him as one.

The defense hurried forward. "I've got Booker!" Alex called as he aligned himself with a shaggy-haired boy. One by one, the four other defenders marked up with their men. Paul, Julian noticed, was the last to be claimed. He saw why a moment later.

Paul dribbled on an angle toward the right corner. He kept himself between the ball and Skeeter, who matched him step for step. Then suddenly, Paul stopped short. Skeeter planted his feet on the floor a moment before Paul charged forward. Julian expected Paul to dodge around Skeeter. Instead, the center plowed right into him, catching him hard in the chest with a dropped shoulder!

Skeeter flew backward. He landed with a dull thud and skidded across the shiny wood floor.

Julian leaped to his feet. He expected Coach Boyd to blow his whistle and stop the play. Paul had caused a flagrant offensive foul, after all, knocking into Skeeter when Skeeter wasn't moving. At the very least, he should make sure Skeeter wasn't hurt.

Instead, the coach kept his eye on his son, clapping as Paul barreled to the basket for an easy layup. None of the other defenders challenged the center. And none of the other offensive players bothered to cut to the hoop. It was as if they all knew exactly what Paul was going to do and they just let him do it.

"Okay, nicely done!" the coach praised. "Set up again. This time, Paul, pass the ball around a few times before taking your shot."

Julian couldn't believe his ears. The coach had just told the defense who would be taking the shot. He'd also told the offense not to bother shooting!

What kind of crazy team is this? he wondered. And then he asked himself something else. *Do I really want to be part of it?*

The coach called his name then. "Okay, Pryce, you're in for Riley."

He stood up, surprised. He'd been certain he'd finish the rest of practice on the bench. Then he saw why he was going in. Riley was limping, an angry red mark blooming near his knee!

"What happened?" he asked in a low voice as the two boys changed places.

"Tripped over Paul's foot," Riley mumbled. "At least, that's what the coach saw."

"Pryce! Now or never!"

Julian ran onto the court and took a position near

the baseline to the right of the hoop. Anger seethed through him.

If Paul tries any funny stuff with me, he thought, *he's in for a big surprise!*

The offense lined up at center court again. A short boy named Murdock — Julian wasn't sure if it was his first or last name — had the ball. Steve-o stuck to him like glue and drove him to the left sideline.

Murdock got rid of the ball soon after with a sharp bounce pass to Booker. Booker didn't even bother to dribble. He just sent it to Will, a forward, who passed it back to Murdock. Murdock dribbled twice and then, predictably, looked for Paul.

That's when Julian made his move. He dashed forward, intercepted Murdock's pass, and dribbled right between Paul and Will! All the other boys stood as still as statues, mouths open. If it had been a real game situation, Julian would have made it all the way to the opposite hoop unchallenged.

Instead, he drew up after a few steps and turned back. He didn't expect Coach Boyd to praise his quick hands. But he didn't expect what he did hear, either.

"Pryce, you're new here so I guess that's why you didn't understand the drill," Coach Boyd said tightly.

"We're working on *offense* here, not *defense*. Ball, please." He held out his hand.

Less than a week earlier, Julian had told the Tornadoes that he wasn't a quitter. But right now, he was sorely tempted to slam the ball down and walk away from the Warriors for good.

Then he caught Alex staring at him with a look of admiration mixed with a hint of amusement. *You did it!* that look seemed to say.

And I'll do it again, Julian decided then and there. *Coach Boyd and his precious son need to learn that one player doesn't make up an entire team, no matter how good he thinks he is!*

So rather than storming off, Julian carefully placed the ball in the coach's hand. "Sorry, coach," he said politely. "I didn't understand what was happening. But now I do. You made it very clear, actually. Thank you."

Coach Boyd locked eyes with Julian for a long moment. Then he cleared his throat and said, "Good. However, our court time is over. That's it for today, Warriors. See you tomorrow."

11

Julian fumed the whole walk home. His mother was putting dinner on the table when he stormed in the door.

"Well!" she exclaimed when she saw his face. "Do I dare ask how your first practice as a Warrior went?"

Julian flopped into a chair across from Megan. He let out an exasperated sigh. "It was awful! The coach plays favorites like you wouldn't believe!"

Mr. Pryce came in just in time to hear Julian's reply. "What do you mean?" he asked as he slid into another chair.

"He was so busy working with the starting lineup that he barely glanced my way," Julian informed him. "And when he did, he criticized what I was doing or didn't say anything at all about my playing!"

Megan snickered.

"What's so funny?" Julian demanded.

"Oh, nothing," Megan said. "It's just, well, you came home from your first practice with the Tornadoes full of complaints, too. Remember?"

Julian started to protest but his mother cut him off.

"She's right, Julian," she said. "Your teammates couldn't do anything right, they were all losers, they expected you to shoulder all the responsibility, and so on and so forth."

"But this is different!" Julian cried. "Coach Boyd —"

"— was kind enough to allow you on his team mid-season," Mr. Pryce interrupted. "What did you expect him to do? Bump out his starting center to put you in?"

"No!" Julian felt his frustration mount. "But he did-n't even give me a chance to show what I can do! I'm telling you, he ignored me all practice!"

Mr. and Mrs. Pryce exchanged looks. Megan rolled her eyes.

"You don't believe me, do you?" Julian cried incredulously.

"I believe that *you* believe that's what happened," Mrs. Pryce said in a soothing voice. "But isn't it possible that you're upset for another reason?"

Julian flung up his hands in disgust. "What other reason could there be?"

Megan answered. "Maybe you're upset because for the first time in a long time you're not the star of the show."

Megan's comment hit Julian like a slap in the face. He shoved back in his chair, rushed out of the room, and ran up the stairs to his bedroom.

"I hate it here!" he cried, slamming the door behind him.

Crash! The framed photograph of the Tornadoes fell from the wall. The glass splintered into sharp shards when it hit the floor. Julian picked it up and stared at the distorted image of his friends.

"Great," he muttered, laying the broken picture on his dresser.

Then he thought of something. He opened the top dresser drawer. Inside was the box of candies from Cutler's. He lifted the lid, grabbed several drops, and stuffed them into his mouth. He barely tasted the chocolate peanut butter treats yet he kept eating. Over and over his hand dipped into the box until a third of the drops were gone.

He sank down onto his bed. The candy churned in his stomach, mixing with his anger and frustration. He lay down and closed his eyes, willing the nausea to pass.

There was a soft knock on his door. He grunted but didn't move. The door creaked open.

"You have a visitor," his mother said.

"Who is it?"

"It's Alex," a different voice said.

Julian's eyes flew open in surprise. "Uh, hi. What're you doing here?"

Alex stepped into the room. "My mom and I live a few doors down. We brought you guys some brownies. I thought maybe you'd like to hang out or something. But maybe you'd rather be alone?"

"Nah, come on in. I'm just . . ." He sighed.

"Bummed out? Confused? So angry you could spit — or slam doors?" Alex guessed.

Julian nodded. "Yeah, all those things."

Alex sat on the floor and stretched out his legs. "Welcome to the club."

Julian closed the door and turned to look at Alex. "It wasn't just my imagination, was it? Coach Boyd *was* ignoring me — ignoring us?"

"If by 'us' you mean the nonstarters, yeah."

"How can you stand it?" Julian burst out.

Alex shook his head. "Good question. The thing is, Coach Boyd wasn't that way last year. We all saw equal playing time, and practices were for the whole team."

Julian picked up his autographed basketball and tossed it from hand to hand. "So what happened to change that?"

Alex screwed up his face as if trying to decide how best to explain it. "You've heard of Kobe Bryant, LeBron James, Kevin Garnett, right?"

"Of course! They're all superstars in the NBA."

"Right. And they have something else in common too."

Julian nodded. "They were all drafted into the pros right out of high school."

Suddenly, he remembered the argument he'd overheard between the high school coach and Coach Boyd. Understanding struck him like a thunderbolt. "That's what the coach hopes will happen with his sons, isn't it?"

Alex shot a finger gun at Julian. "Bingo! He sent Peter and Paul to an exclusive basketball camp this past summer. I guess they performed well enough to impress a few people. Now Coach Boyd is pushing for them to get as much playing time as they can. The more coverage they get in the papers and local media, the more likely he thinks it'll be that the NBA scouts will hear about them, and come calling."

Julian remembered what Alex had said about being

Web-worthy. He could understand why the coach might think his plan could pay off. "Are they really that good?" Julian asked.

Alex shrugged. "Peter is better than average, I guess. But is he or Paul NBA material?" He shook his head. "As far as Paul's concerned, at least, I'd have to say his ego is greater than his talent."

Julian got up and paced the room, stopping near his dresser. "So we're stuck sitting on the bench while he gets all the playing time."

"Unless something changes, probably."

The two boys were silent as they contemplated that fact. Julian, deep in thought, absently plucked another Triple Chocolate Peanut Butter Drop from the box and popped it into his mouth.

"What are those things, anyway?" Alex asked. Julian told him about the candy and then offered him some. Alex accepted and chewed appreciatively. "Wow. These are awesome. Got any more?"

Julian laughed ruefully. "Not as many as I had earlier tonight." He handed Alex the box. "Maybe I should bring the rest to practice tomorrow. Then you and I and the other nonstarters will have something to do — eat!"

He had meant it as a joke, of course, but to his surprise, Alex shook his head vigorously. "Don't bring them, whatever you do! Or anything that has peanut butter or peanuts in it."

"Why not?"

"Paul is allergic to peanuts," Alex informed him. "Even a whiff of something with peanuts makes him sick."

Julian had heard of other kids with food allergies. But this was the first one he'd been around. To show Alex that he understood how serious the condition was, he closed the lid on the box and shut the dresser drawer. As he did, his cell phone suddenly chirped. He picked it up and looked at it.

"WR U @?" asked a text message. He grinned. The message was from Grady!

Julian was dying to talk to his old friend. But he thought it would be rude to start texting, or dial Grady's house, with Alex sitting there. So instead, he texted just a short message — CL U L8R, or Call You Later.

He had just finished when Alex's mother appeared to say it was time for her and Alex to go.

Julian pocketed his phone and followed Alex downstairs. "Hey, man, thanks for coming over."

"See you in school tomorrow, and the court tomorrow afternoon!" Alex replied.

Mr. Pryce closed the door after them. Then he turned and fixed Julian with a serious eye. "Sit down, son. I have something I want to say to you."

12

Julian sat at the kitchen table. He started to apologize for storming off. His father stopped him.

"We're the ones who should be apologizing to you," he said.

"Huh?"

Mrs. Pryce sat next to him. "It seems you were telling us the truth about Coach Boyd. Mrs. Harrison has seen it herself. In fact, she's been considering filing a complaint. Alex convinced her not to."

Julian understood why Alex didn't want his mother involved. It could be embarrassing to have a parent — even one trying to help — fight your battles.

"Anyway," Mr. Pryce said, "if you'd rather not play for Coach Boyd and the Warriors, we won't keep you from quitting. You could always join another team next season."

Julian was tempted. But then he thought about Alex

and the others. Somehow, he felt he'd be letting them down if he jumped ship. And then there was Coach Valenti, who had gone out of his way to get him on the team in the first place. How would the coach feel when he learned Julian had attended only one practice, and then quit?

So he shook his head. "I'll stick with the Warriors," he said. "Who knows? Maybe I'll do something to catch Coach Boyd's attention!"

Just then, his stomach gave a loud growl.

"Well, that caught *my* attention, anyway!" Mrs. Pryce said with a laugh. She opened the stove and handed him a hot plate of food. "I saved your supper, if you're hungry. And there are brownies for dessert."

Julian grimaced at the thought of more chocolate. "Just supper, please," he said, pulling his plate closer. "And thanks, Mom, Dad, for understanding."

Julian ate his supper in a flash. Then he hurried back to his room and dialed Grady's number. He liked texting, but sometimes he preferred a real, live conversation. Besides, nothing could make him feel better than making Grady laugh.

That's just what happened too. Now that he was over his anger, he was able to joke about his first lousy practice with the Warriors. When he got to the part about stealing the ball from Paul, Grady howled with laughter.

"Man, I would have loved to see the expression on that bozo's face when you did that! Priceless!"

Julian grinned. "I wish I'd checked it out myself. But I was too busy being yelled at by the coach." Then his grin faded. "Tell me something, Grady, and I want the truth. Was I as much of a jerk to you earlier this season as Paul is being to me now?"

To his relief, Grady laughed again. "I didn't like you very much for a while. But I was pretty sure you'd come around eventually."

"Thanks to Barry, I did. How is his physical therapy coming along?" Since his accident, Barry had been working with a therapist, trying to regain the use of his bad leg.

Grady was quiet for so long Julian that grew nervous. "He's okay, isn't he?"

"Oh, yeah, Barry's fine," Grady answered. "He told me he gave you the candy before you left, by the way. Have you had any yet?"

"Yeah, like a third of it," Julian confessed.

"Sheesh! I didn't know you were such a pig!"

The boys chatted a while longer and then Grady said he had to go finish his homework. "It was good talking to you, Jools."

It was only after Julian had hung up that he realized Grady had never really answered his question about Barry's progress.

Could Grady be hiding something from me? he wondered. *And if so, why?*

He yawned suddenly. A quick glance at the clock showed him that it was near his bedtime. "I'm just imagining things," he said as he changed into a T-shirt and flannel pants. "Grady said Barry was fine. So he must be fine."

Julian went to bed soon after that. He awoke the next morning feeling refreshed and determined to face head-on whatever challenges came that day.

The hours at school passed without a problem; he knew where his classrooms were, who his teachers were, and knew a few of his classmates too. But when he walked onto the basketball court that afternoon, his determination faltered.

Once again, Coach Boyd separated the team into two groups, one of starters, one of subs. Once again, Julian was put in with the subs. Even though he'd been expecting it, he couldn't help resenting his placement with the less-talented players.

That resentment grew whenever he watched the starters practice. There were some good players on that side of the court. But as far as he could tell, their skills were going to waste. The coach seemed to have designed nearly every play with one goal in mind: get the ball to Paul!

Julian worked hard not to let his frustration get the better of him during that practice or the ones that followed in the next two days. Instead, he put his energy into the drills he and the other subs ran. But when it came time for his first game in a Warriors uniform, the cold hard reality of his situation sank in completely.

He was a benchwarmer.

13

"Let's go, Warriors!"

The cheers rang out from the fans scattered throughout the bleachers of the gymnasium. Julian smoothed the slippery red fabric of his new jersey and then joined his teammates circling the court for a few warm-up laps.

"Come on, Pryce, shake a leg! Or do I have to come down there and show you how it's done?"

Julian jerked his head around. He knew that voice — Barry! He searched the stands, looking for a kid sitting with his bound leg propped up next to a pair of crutches. That's why he missed Barry at first; his old friend wasn't sitting at all, he was standing on two legs!

Julian's jaw dropped. "No way!" he called. "Awesome!"

Barry heard Julian's cry and grinned from ear to ear.

But when he moved to sit down, Julian noticed he still favored his left leg.

Julian realized then that although Barry's injured leg was better, it wasn't healed completely. Still, he'd come a long way in the two weeks since Julian had last seen him! It made him wonder what else he'd missed back home — and what he'd keep missing every day.

Paul Boyd drew alongside him then. "Got a fan in the stands, huh, Pryce?" he sneered. "Big deal. Seen my fan club lately?" He jerked his chin toward another section of the bleachers.

Julian looked and saw two dozen middle school kids sitting together. Some of them held signs saying "Go, Paul!" When the team ran by them, they started chanting. "Paul Boyd, he's our man! If he can't do it, no one can!"

I wouldn't be so sure about that, Julian thought. *Give me a chance, and I'll give you someone else to cheer about!*

By then, the other team had arrived. The Suns wore yellow uniforms as brilliant as their team name. They took over one half of the court and began doing layup drills. After a minute, the Warriors did the same at their end of the court.

A buzzer sounded soon after to alert the teams that the game was about to begin.

"All right, Jools, show 'em what you can do!" Julian heard Barry yell.

"Yeah, *Jools*," Paul mimicked, "show 'em how good you are at riding the pine!"

Julian glowered but didn't say a word. He knew he'd get into the game at some point. He had to; it was the league regulation. And when he did, he'd make the most of every second he played.

For now, however, he had to swallow his pride and sit with the other subs. He risked a glance at Barry, expecting his friend to look surprised, or worse, amused. But Barry just smiled and gave him a thumbs-up sign.

The game started a moment later. Paul sauntered onto the floor and took up his position in the center circle. The Suns center did the same. The ref stood between them with the ball.

Julian leaned forward. He loved the second before the tip-off. Even now, sitting on the bench, his body tensed, ready to spring like a coil suddenly let loose.

Tweet!

The whistle blew. The ball soared from the ref's fingertips into the air between the centers. Paul jumped high — but the Suns center jumped higher. With a mighty wallop, he sent the ball sizzling down into his guard's hands.

The Sun guard didn't hold it for long. After two dribbles, he passed up the court to another guard. The Warriors, meanwhile, rushed back on defense.

"Two-one-two!" Coach Boyd shouted.

Julian looked at him in surprise. *He's just telling them what zone to run now? Shouldn't he have done that before the game?*

The Warriors hesitated for just a split second before hurrying to their positions. But that second was enough for the Suns guard to thread a path right through them. Then — *thump! swish!* — he banked in a beautiful shot three feet from the hoop.

The whole move was so smooth that Julian almost jumped to his feet to applaud. Luckily, he remembered at the last moment that he was playing for the other team!

Booker, the Warriors guard, took the ball under the basket. He passed to Murdock, who dribbled quickly down the floor.

"FX 1!" Murdock cried as he crossed the center line. "FX 1!"

FX 1? Julian thought. *What the heck is that?*

The play's setup found Murdock bringing the ball to

the right top corner of the key. Booker took the opposite corner. Paul was in the right corner on the baseline. Jackson, one of the forwards, was in the other while Will, the second forward, sprinted to the far left edge of the three-point arc.

The Suns, meanwhile, positioned themselves in a one-two-two zone, arms raised, legs wide, in classic defensive poses. Still, they were one step behind the Warriors when the play unfolded.

Whap! Murdock slapped the ball with the palm of his hand to signal the play's start. Then he passed over to Booker and ran down to set a pick on the Sun closest to Paul. Jackson came across the court, too, to set a second screen.

Free from defenders, Paul rolled out of his slot and dashed in front of the hoop. Will crossed behind him. Paul held up his hands, clearly looking for a pass from Booker.

But a Sun was covering Booker too well. A pass could have been easily picked off. Booker dribbled back a few steps. The defender followed, but not soon enough. With lightning-quick speed, Booker switched from a right-hand dribble to a left-hand dribble. He made a beeline for left side of the court.

Again, the defender followed. He was so intent on watching the ball that he didn't see Paul.

Pick! Set a pick for Booker! Julian urged silently. All Paul needed to do was put his body in the defender's way. The defender would crash into him — and Booker could keep dribbling past on his way to the hoop and a possible basket.

But Paul either didn't see that opportunity or chose to ignore it. He sidled farther away from the hoop and clapped his hands. The sound drew the defender's attention — more than one defender, actually. Suddenly, three players were surrounding Paul and Booker. Booker panicked and stopped his dribble. Now they were trapped!

14

A split second passed with both Paul and Booker standing as if frozen.

Julian jumped to his feet. "Help him out, Paul!" he cried.

Maybe Paul heard him. Or maybe he'd already made up his mind to do just that. In any event, he took one step toward Booker. When the closest Sun mirrored his move, Paul charged the other way, toward the hoop.

The movement must have distracted the other two defenders, for suddenly, Booker twisted between them and bounced a pass to Paul. Paul caught it, turned to the hoop, jumped — and clanged a mighty brick off the rim!

The ball ricocheted high in the air. Paul, Will, and Jackson jockeyed with three Suns for the best positions for the rebound. Paul and the Suns tall center reached it first. The ball danced between their fingertips before finally coming to land in the Sun's hands.

The Sun didn't hesitate. With a practiced move, he hurled an outlet pass to his guard, who was waiting near the sideline. The guard caught it and raced down the court, dribbling madly. So madly, in fact, that he lost control of the ball! It flew out of his hands and into the nearby bleachers.

Tweet! The referee blew a short blast on his whistle and then hurried to retrieve the ball.

That was a lucky break, Julian thought. *A few more steps and he would have been in firing range!*

The Suns' turnover ended with a Warrior basket. Tie score, 2–2, with four minutes remaining in the first eight-minute quarter.

Julian shifted on the bench. He'd never realized how hard wooden bleachers could be. Of course, he'd never spent so much time sitting on one before, at least not during a game.

The play moved from the Suns' end of the court to the Warriors', and back again. The Suns scored a few buckets, but the Warriors drained some of their own, including a steady-handed free throw from Jackson that swished the net strings. When the buzzer sounded, the score stood at Suns 12, Warriors 9.

Julian stood up and applauded along with his team-mates. He glanced at the stands to where Barry was sitting. Barry gave him a smile. Then he pointed from Julian to the court and shrugged. "So, when are you getting in?" those gestures seemed to ask.

Julian looked away. If that was the question, he did-n't know the answer.

He still didn't know the answer when the halftime buzzer went off. But he did know something else — he absolutely *hated* sitting on the sidelines!

Every muscle in his body ached from the tension of watching when he wanted to be playing. He longed for the sting of the ball as it hit his hands, for the feel of sweat of pouring down his face. He missed the thud of the blood pumping through his veins and the breath-lessness that came with running up and down the court. Heck, he even missed the squeak of his sneak-ers on the polished wood!

One thing's for sure, he thought. *I'll never take play-ing for granted again!*

"Warriors!" Coach Boyd's angry shout made Julian start. "In the far corner! *Now!*"

Julian grimaced. He knew why the coach was upset. The Warriors were behind 23 to 18. Julian was pretty sure Paul had made only five of those points — not enough to please his father, no doubt. He grabbed his water bottle and followed his teammates to the end of the court.

Paul sat next to the coach, a thick towel draped over his shoulders. As Coach Boyd gave his players a pep talk — *more like a talking to*, Julian thought — Paul used the towel to wipe perspiration from his face and neck.

Julian bit his lip. He had a towel just like that in the duffel bag he'd stowed behind his seat. Even though his mother washed the towel after every game, Julian liked to imagine that it held a bit of the sweat it had collected from those matches — mementos of each one he'd played.

Mom won't have to wash that towel after this game, he thought ruefully.

"Pryce!"

Julian's head snapped up at the sound of Coach Boyd calling his name.

"I hope you've been paying attention," the coach said, "because you're going in at the start of the second half."

Julian blinked in surprise and then nodded. "Yes, sir," he said. "I — I won't let you down, sir!"

Coach Boyd pressed his lips together in a thin line

but he didn't reply. He named a few other subs going in with Julian, including Skeeter and Alex at guard. Then the referee called over that the second half was going to begin in a few minutes.

"All right, Warriors," Coach Boyd growled. "Let's see you put a cloud over those Suns! Hands in the middle and . . . go Warriors!"

Julian and the others hurried to the court for some warm-up drills. The movement loosened Julian's muscles and for the first time that afternoon, he felt himself relax.

That feeling lasted only a few seconds after the starters returned to the bench. To his shock, Paul wasn't among them!

Maybe he didn't hear his father say I was starting this quarter, he thought. But when he tried to tell Paul as much, Paul just laughed.

"Nice try!" he said.

"But—"

"But nothing!" Paul cut in. "You may be in the game, but not at center. I'm the only center on this team. You're in for Will. At forward!"

15

Forward?!" Julian's mouth dropped open in horror. "But I don't know what to do at forward!"

Paul rolled his eyes. "Well, I hope you're a fast learner, then, because that's your position for the next few minutes."

"Ready, Warriors?" the referee called just then.

Paul nodded. Then, without a backward glance at Julian, he hurried off for the opening throw-in. Julian hesitated at mid-court, unsure of where to go or what to do. Then Jackson appeared at his side.

"Keep an eye on number 13 over there, okay?" the freckled-faced forward said to Julian. "Will said he's got a good shot, and he's on your side of the zone — the left baseline corner of the two-one-two zone. If we get the ball, run down the side to the left corner."

"Thanks, Jackson," Julian said gratefully. "But what do I do on offense?"

Jackson gave a short laugh. "Do what the rest of us do — get the ball to Paul!"

Julian was surprised to hear bitterness in Jackson's voice. For the first time, it occurred to him that maybe the other Warrior starters didn't care for Coach Boyd's strategy any more than he and the subs did. But there wasn't time to ask about that now. The game was about to resume, and he needed to get into position!

The referee gave the Suns guard the ball and blew the whistle. The guard immediately bounced a pass to a forward, who returned it just as quickly.

Julian raced down to the left corner of the zone defense. He raised his hands in the air and watched the ball carrier like a hawk. Would the guard drive to the hoop? Take a jump shot? Or would he pass to set up a play?

A movement to his right caught his eye. A Sun player had slipped behind Jackson along the baseline. Now he was turning to look at the guard.

He's waiting for a pass! The thought struck Julian just as the guard stopped his dribble. Julian lunged to put himself between the Sun and the ball. He stretched out his hand, reaching, reaching — *whap!*

84

His palm met the ball squarely and deflected the ball away from the waiting Sun! Even better, the ball bounced at Skeeter's feet!

Skeeter scooped it up, held it for a second, and then put it to the floor with a soft, controlled fingertip dribble. Players rushed past him, Warriors to get down on offense, Suns to set up on defense.

Julian hurried to the left corner, as Jackson had instructed him to do. Once there, however, he was at a loss. *What am I supposed to do now?*

Luckily, Skeeter was taking his time bringing the ball down the court. Those precious seconds gave Julian a chance to think — and to remember what the forwards on his old team used to do.

Cut in and out of the key, move toward the ball, set picks, and shoot! It wasn't that different from what he did at center, actually.

He danced a few steps into the paint. That maneuver drew his defender to him. So he backpedaled out again. His defender didn't follow. Instead, the Sun moved to stay close to Paul.

They've figured out that Paul is the one taking the shots! Julian suddenly realized. *They don't think I'm a scoring threat!* He smiled inwardly. *Well, they'd be wrong about that! If I can just get the ball . . .*

It was as if Skeeter had read his mind, for at that moment, he stopped his dribble and fired a pass into Julian's hands.

Paul signaled for the ball. But two Suns were covering him so completely that any attempted pass would end up in a turnover.

Julian, on the other hand, was wide open. He paused and then shot.

The ball arced high above the Suns and the Warriors. It seemed to hang in the air before beginning its descent. When it did come down, it was directly over the hoop.

Fwing! Nothing but net! Two points!

"Whoo-hoo, Jools! Way to go!" Barry's voice rang out loud and clear above the smattering of applause.

Julian grinned as he ran past the stands to get on defense. "Who's that kid?" he heard someone ask.

"No clue," was the reply. "But he's got a sweet shot!"

Hearing the exchange made Julian's heart soar with hope. Maybe now Coach Boyd would use him more often!

But a split second later, his hopes were dashed. Will and Booker were crouching by the check-in table. At the next whistle, they jumped up and ran onto the court. Julian knew what Will was going to say even as the words were coming out of his mouth.

"Pryce! I'm in for you!" Will called.

As Julian jogged off the floor, he glanced at the game clock. Only three minutes of the third quarter had passed!

Three minutes! That was all?

Alex had come out too. Now he slid up next to Julian. "Awesome shot, man," he murmured. "Too bad it got you benched."

Julian looked at him sideways. "I would have passed to Paul if he'd been open!" he replied just as quietly. "But the ball would have been picked off if I'd tried. I had the shot so I took it. Doesn't the coach think a basket is better than a turnover?"

Alex sighed. "Of course he does. But as far as he's concerned, the two points you made are two points Paul *didn't* make. It's not about winning the game — it's about making his son look good."

Julian drummed his fingers on his legs in frustration. "Well, that's just flat out wrong."

"Tell me something I *don't* know," Alex agreed. "*All* of us Warriors know. But what can we do about it — except quit?"

Julian shook his head. "Quitting isn't the answer. He can just replace us with other players. He needs to see that what he's doing isn't right if anything is going to change!"

Alex shrugged. "Sure, that'd be great. But the question is, how can we make him see?"

Julian stared out at the court. Players were running up and down, blurs of red and yellow. "If he just wasn't so focused on Paul all the time, maybe he would see that we're all pretty good," he said finally. "But I don't see how we can possibly change that. Not if Paul stays on the court, anyway!"

16

Julian got back into the game midway through the fourth quarter. By that time, the Warriors were behind by eight points. He got his hands on the ball a few times, but took and made just one shot. When the final buzzer sounded, the Suns had outshone the Warriors, 46 to 40.

Julian followed his teammates through the hand-slap ritual. But instead of joining them in the locker room right away, he hurried to the stands to see Barry. Megan, Barry's parents, and his parents were there too.

"Hey! Good game!" Barry said.

Julian laughed mirthlessly. "Yeah, right. I'm sorry you came all this way just to see me ride the pine."

"Okay, so that was lousy. But forget about you." Barry stood up and held his arms wide. "Check this out! No crutches!"

Julian laughed again, but this time it was with real happiness. "I know! I saw you earlier! That is great!"

"Thanks," Barry said. "I'm still a long way from rejoining the Tornadoes, but at least I can get around on my own two feet." But when he tried to climb out of the bleachers, he stumbled. Julian caught him before he fell.

"Rats," Barry growled. "I thought I could do that. I did it at halftime! Really!"

"He did," Megan agreed. "I started to help him but he said he wanted to hide the —"

Barry cleared his throat loudly. Megan widened her eyes as if remembering something and stopped talking.

Julian looked from one to the other suspiciously. "He wanted to hide the what?"

"Hide the — the crutches I still have to carry with me," Barry said. "So, are you going to get your stuff? Your folks invited us to see your new house."

Julian didn't move. "Why do I get the impression you two are up to something?"

Megan and Barry shrugged but seemed to be holding back laughter.

"Fine, don't tell me!" Julian left the stands then to

collect his duffel bag. He had stowed it in the seats behind the team bench. There were other bags there too. He was reaching for his when another hand grabbed it first.

"You going to steal my stuff now, just like you steal my points?" Paul hissed.

Julian narrowed his eyes. "Last I checked, points belong to the team, not one player! And this is my bag, not yours!" He wrapped his hands around the duffel's straps and tried to pull it up from the seat.

Paul abruptly sat on the bag, jerking it out of Julian's hands as he did. "Dude, I'm telling you, this is mine! Unless your initials changed from J. P. to P. B.?" He pointed to some lettering on the bag's side that Julian had failed to notice before.

Julian's face turned hot. "Sorry," he muttered. He searched the seats and found his own duffel. It was identical to Paul's, minus the lettering. "My bad."

Paul stood up and plumped his squashed duffel back into form. Then he swung it over his shoulder and stormed away without another word.

Julian watched him go before hurrying to rejoin his family and friends.

"What was that all about?" Barry asked.

"Nothing important," Julian answered. "Come on. Let's get back to my house. I want to grab a shower and forget about this whole stupid afternoon!"

It turned out that Barry and his folks couldn't come to the Pryce's house after all.

"It's a school day tomorrow," Mr. Streeter reminded Barry when his son protested. "For you and for Julian."

Mrs. Pryce and Mrs. Streeter looked just as disappointed as their sons. But they promised the boys they'd all get together as soon as possible.

"At least you have something to remember me by," Barry said in the parking lot.

"What do you mean?" Julian asked, puzzled. Then he laughed. "Oh, if you mean the chocolate peanut butter drops, I've already eaten most of them." He put his hand to his heart. "But I swear I think of you and the guys every time I eat one! Really!"

Barry grinned. "Suuure you do! I wasn't talking about those drops, though."

"What were you talking about then?"

Barry waggled his eyebrows. "Oh, you'll find out soon enough, I'm sure!" He climbed into his parents' car before Julian could ask him anything more.

Julian waved until the car was out of sight. Then he

tossed his duffel bag into the trunk of the Pryce's car, got into the backseat, and put on his seat belt. "I'm ready to go home," he said.

Mr. Pryce started the motor and then glanced at him over the seat. "I think that's the first time any of us have called our new house 'home.' Maybe we're starting to think of it that way at last?" He sounded hopeful.

"Maybe," Julian said. But he only said it because he knew his father needed to hear it. Deep down, he would have given anything to still be living in their old house, in their old neighborhood — and to be part of the team made up of kids he called friends.

Suddenly, there was a knock on his window. He looked up, startled, to see Alex and Jackson standing there. He pushed the button on his door and the glass rolled down.

"Uh, hey guys, what's up?"

"We're going to get some pizza," Alex said. "Want to come?"

Julian blinked. "I — really?"

Jackson nodded. "Come on, everyone's hoping you'll show!"

"Can I, Mom?" Julian asked.

Mrs. Pryce beamed at him. "Sure!" She asked the

boys the name of the place and told Julian she'd pick him up there in two hours. "And honey?" she added as Julian got out of the car. "Have fun!"

Julian looked to where Alex and Jackson waited. "Thanks. I think I will!"

17

Julian did have fun with Alex and Jackson at the pizza place. Booker and Skeeter were there too. The five of them shared a large pepperoni pie and played video games. When his mother came to pick him up, he was sorry to leave.

"Hey, I'll see you at school tomorrow," he called.

"You had a good time?" Mrs. Pryce asked.

"Yeah. Those guys are pretty cool."

His mother was quiet for a few minutes. Then she said, "So, you think you'll survive living here?"

Julian stared out his window at the passing houses. A small smile played around his lips. "I think so. Now that I've made a couple of friends — yeah, I think I'll do just fine here."

Back home, Mrs. Pryce disappeared into the laundry room. Julian went to his bedroom.

The room didn't feel quite as strange as it had at first. His books were on his bookshelf, his desk was set up with his computer, and his closet held a lot of his clothes. But one important thing was missing — friends. His old bedroom had been smaller, but it was always big enough for Grady, Barry, and other friends to hang out in.

Julian opened the top drawer of his dresser and plucked the few last Cutler's candies from the box.

"I'm thinking of you guys," he whispered.

As he chewed, he looked around his room. He tried to imagine his old friends sitting in it. Instead, someone else came to mind: Alex. It wasn't surprising, really — Alex had already been there, after all. But it was something more, Julian thought.

Alex had treated him like a friend, right from the start.

A sudden memory struck Julian then. It was the Tornadoes' first practice. Julian was just realizing that he was the only returning starter when Mick Reiss, the new kid, had come onto the court. Grady had greeted Mick warmly and made him feel welcome. Julian, on the other hand, had refused to have anything to do with him — at first, at least.

Alex treated me just like Grady treated Mick, he

thought. *And Paul . . . is treating me just like I treated Mick!*

An idea started forming in his mind. He lay down on his bed, crossed his legs, and jogged his foot up and down.

Mick and I are friends now because Grady made me see I was acting like a jerk toward him. Maybe . . . maybe Alex could do the same with Paul and me. It was worth a shot, he figured.

Julian awoke early the next morning, ate a big breakfast of cereal and toast, and then hurried to school. He caught up with Alex near his locker. But when he started to ask him to help smooth the way with Paul, Alex looked at him in confusion.

"Didn't you hear? Paul's in the hospital!"

Julian blinked in surprise. "What? What happened?"

Alex closed his locker with a slam. "He went into anaphylactic shock on the car ride home from the game last night."

"Ana-what?"

"Anaphylactic shock. Remember how I told you he's severely allergic to peanuts?"

Julian nodded.

"Well, he must have come into contact with some. His lips and face turned puffy. His skin broke out in itchy red patches. His tongue swelled up and his throat started to close. He couldn't breathe!"

Julian's hand crept to his neck. Paul must have been terrified! "Is he okay?"

Alex bit his lip. "It was a pretty bad reaction. But it could have been a whole lot worse. Luckily, Coach Boyd keeps a shot of the medicine Paul needs with him at all times. It's called epinephrine, I think. The coach gave Paul the shot and then drove him to the emergency room. The doctors are keeping Paul for a day just to be sure he's all right."

"Wow. That's unreal." He and Alex started walking down the hallway to their first class. "Where did the peanuts come from, anyway?"

"No one knows how he got exposed." Alex shifted his books from one arm to the other. "Anyway, since you didn't know about Paul, I'm guessing you didn't hear that practice is canceled today, either."

Julian shook his head.

"Jackson and I are going to visit him in the hospital after school," Alex said. "You want to come?"

Julian hesitated. "You think he'd be okay with that? If you hadn't noticed, we aren't the best of buddies!"

Alex smiled. "You're hoping to change that though, right? Now's your chance — after all, he's confined to a hospital bed so he'll be a captive audience!"

"Well, when you put it that way," Julian said, laughing, "sure, I'll come this afternoon."

18

When Julian walked into Paul's hospital room later that day, he felt as if he'd been transported back in time. After all, less than three months ago he'd walked into a similar room, to visit Barry. Paul looked a whole lot better than Barry had, however. Barry's head had been wrapped in gauze, his broken limbs had been encased in plaster casts, and tubes had run into his arms.

Paul, meanwhile, was just hooked up to a single intravenous drip. Yet Julian could tell he had been through an ordeal. There were dark circles under his eyes. His skin looked blotchy. When he spoke, his voice was raspy.

"What's *he* doing here?" he asked, jutting his chin in Julian's direction.

Any sympathy Julian had felt vanished. He turned to leave when Alex stopped him.

"He's here because he's your teammate," Alex replied

calmly. "Now stop being a jerk or I'll have an orderly bring you a peanut butter and jelly sandwich for lunch!"

Julian sucked in his breath. He was sure Paul would order them all from the room.

But to his amazement, Paul chuckled. "Been a while since you talked to me that way," he said.

Alex pulled up a chair next to the bed and sat down. "Yeah, well, it's been a while since you noticed I existed!"

Julian looked from one boy to the other and then tugged Jackson to one side. "Am I missing something here?" he whispered.

Jackson nodded. "Alex and Paul are best friends. Or they used to be, anyway, until Coach Boyd decided Paul was going to be the next NBA superstar. Since then, Paul's done nothing but play basketball. He never gets to hang out with us anymore. When he's not at practice, he's working on his shot. Or he's lifting weights. Or running on a track. Or downing special protein bars to get big and strong."

"Wow," Julian said. "He must really like basketball."

Jackson shrugged as if to say maybe he did, maybe he didn't, before wandering over to the bed. Julian hesitated, and then joined the others.

"So did they find out what caused the attack?" Alex was asking Paul.

"My mom did, when she was cleaning out my duffel bag this morning," Paul answered. "My towel had these weird smudges all over it. Turns out the smudges were made by chocolate and peanut butter." He laid his head back against his pillow as if he was suddenly exhausted. "I remember wiping my face on the towel on the way home last night. I must have rubbed the peanut butter on me without knowing it."

"Didn't you see the smudges?" Jackson asked.

"It was dark in the car," Paul pointed out.

"How did the candy get in your bag in the first place?" Alex wanted to know.

At that question, Paul shook his head. "Search me. My dad doesn't allow me to eat candy. So someone else must have stuck it in there."

"Who would have done that?"

"Search me," Paul said again. "But it shouldn't be hard to find out because there was a small white box in my duffel bag, too." He screwed up his face as if trying to remember. "The box had a name on it — Culbert's, or Cutter's, something like that. If we can figure out —"

Julian's sharp gasp interrupted whatever Paul was going to say. The other boys stared at him.

"What is it?" Jackson asked.

"N-Nothing," Julian stammered. "I just remembered I have to go somewhere." He backed out of the room and quickly closed the door. Then he leaned against the wall. His mind was racing.

The box didn't say Culbert's or Cutter's. It said *Cutler's*! Chocolate peanut butter drops like the ones he had at home had put Paul in the hospital! But how had the drops gotten into Paul's bag in the first place? He hadn't put them there, and he was the only one who knew about Cutler's and their Triple Chocolate Peanut Butter Drops.

Then his eyes widened. *No, I'm not*, he thought. *Alex knows about them too. What if he thinks I put the candy in Paul's duffel so that Paul would get sick?*

19

Julian ducked into a nearby bathroom and used his cell phone to call his mother. She promised to pick him up in ten minutes. He spent the time hiding in a bathroom. He didn't want to risk running into Alex or Jackson. If Alex had remembered about the candy, he might have told Jackson. Then maybe the two of them would come looking for him — to accuse him of sabotaging their star center.

When he got home, he dashed up to his room and pulled open the top drawer of his dresser. He looked inside and sighed with relief. The nearly empty Cutler's box was still there.

At least I know the box in Paul's duffel bag wasn't mine, he thought. He lay down on his bed and laced his fingers behind his head. *But it doesn't clear up the mystery of where that other one came from!*

He closed his eyes and envisioned the gym as it had looked the day before. He and the other subs had been sitting on the bench. Their duffel bags were on the seats behind them. Paul's fan club was nearby. If someone had slipped something into Paul's duffel, surely they or one of the Warriors would have noticed?

Unless one of Paul's fans had done it? He dismissed the thought as soon as it entered his brain. Fans didn't sabotage their favorite players. They wouldn't have dared with all the Warriors right there, anyway. And since there had always been at least some Warriors there —

Julian sat up abruptly. *That's not true,* he realized. *There were a few minutes when none of the Warriors were on the bench — halftime! Someone could have easily put the candy in Paul's bag when we were all at the far end of the gym!*

He stood up and paced his room. "Okay," he muttered, "I've figured out the *when*. But what about the *who*? And most importantly, the *why*?"

He picked up the photograph of the Tornadoes from the top of his dresser. He looked from Grady to Mick, and then stopped at Barry. "Too bad you didn't see anything yesterday," he said with a sigh.

He put the picture back and stared around his room. Suddenly, his eyes alighted on his duffel bag. When he did, something clicked in his brain.

He had mistaken Paul's duffel bag for his own. What if someone else had too?

The pieces of the puzzle started falling into place. Barry had been at yesterday's game. He had left the stands during halftime to do something secretive. Barry knew that Julian loved Cutler's Triple Chocolate Peanut Butter Drops. And Barry knew what Julian's duffel bag looked like, because it was the same bag he'd had for years!

What if Barry had slipped the box of candy into Paul's bag, thinking the duffel belonged to Julian?

Paul sat on his bag to keep me from taking it, Julian thought. *He must have squashed the box. The box opened and some of the candy spilled out. Then the chocolate smeared all over his towel when he threw the bag over his shoulder!*

"That's got to be what happened!" Julian cried. "And I know how to find out for sure!" He raced out of his room. "Megan! Megan!"

Megan's bedroom door opened. "What're you shouting about?"

"Did you help Barry put a box of Cutler's candy in my duffel bag yesterday?"

Megan grinned. "It's about time you found it! I've been dying for some!"

Julian let out a low whistle. "Dying is what almost happened, all right!"

He told her everything he had figured out. Her eyes grew wide with horror. "Oh, my gosh! Come on, we have to tell Mom."

"And Coach Boyd," Julian added grimly. It wasn't a conversation he was looking forward to.

Fortunately, Mrs. Boyd and Mrs. Pryce were both present when Julian and Megan explained to Coach Boyd what had happened. That made it a little easier to get the words out.

"So you see, sir, it was all just a terrible mistake," Julian finished. "How — how is Paul doing?"

Mrs. Boyd answered. "He's going to be pretty worn out for the next few days. But he'll be fine. He's coming home in a little while, actually."

The coach cleared his throat. "His doctor advised him not to play basketball for a week," he said gruffly. "I guess that means you'll be taking his place until he's ready to return." He didn't look pleased at the idea.

107

Julian stared at his toes. "Um, yes, sir. Whatever you say."

"I'll see you at practice tomorrow afternoon."

Julian nodded. Then he and his mother left.

The phone was ringing when they returned to their house. Julian answered it.

"Julian? It's Alex. There's something I want to know."

Julian gripped the receiver tightly. The suspicion in the other boy's voice had come through loud and clear. He set about removing that suspicion as quickly as he could by telling him everything he'd just told the coach.

Alex was quiet for a long moment. When he spoke again, he sounded relieved. "It all makes sense now! Man, when I realized that the name on the box was Cutler's, not Culbert's or Cutter's . . ."

"You had to have wondered if I had put it in Paul's bag," Julian finished.

"It did cross my mind," Alex admitted. "I even wondered if you'd come to the hospital room to see if your plan had worked. You know, the old 'criminal returning to the scene of the crime' kind of thing."

"Did you — you didn't talk to anyone else about what you thought, did you?" Julian asked.

"No. I wanted to talk to you first. And man, am I glad I did!"

"Me too, especially since Coach Boyd is going to start me in the next game."

Alex whistled. "Can you imagine what the other Warriors would have thought if they believed you'd deliberately put Paul in the hospital? Yikes!"

"Yeah. I wouldn't have lasted too long on the court, I don't think!"

"Are you kidding? I would have led the charge against you!" Alex said. "Instead, I plan to back you up all the way!"

"Thanks, Alex. That means a lot."

And it did.

20

Julian arrived at basketball practice the next day ready to work hard. And he did just that. But he was careful about how he played too — no fancy moves, or tricks, or showboating of any kind. Nothing, in short, that would make his new teammates think he was trying to outshine them, or Paul.

Julian wasn't looking to be the team's new star. He wasn't after glory. He simply wanted to play. To his delight, that's just what he got to do.

Three days after Paul's hospitalization, the Warriors faced the Ravens in a game on their home court. Paul was there, dressed in the team's jersey, but not to play. He sat on the far end of the bench, as if unsure how he fit in.

Julian nudged Alex when he saw that. "Make him take his usual spot, by his dad," he whispered.

"Why?" Alex whispered back.

"Because I don't want him or the coach to think I'm trying to take over his position," Julian told him.

Alex nodded. He went to talk to Paul. A moment later, the lanky center moved to sit near Coach Boyd.

After the warm-ups, the two teams took to the court. Julian's heart raced as he stood in the center circle for the tip-off. It had been more than three weeks since he'd been in this spot. What if he forgot what to do?

He needn't have worried. When the ref blew his whistle and tossed the ball high in the air, Julian leaped after it, just as he'd done countless times before. And, just as he'd done countless times before, he won the tip and sent the ball down on a line to Booker's outstretched hands.

Ten boys thundered down the court to take up their positions. The red-uniformed Warriors danced in and out of the key, looking for a pass from Booker. The Ravens, their black jerseys shimmering under the gym lights, followed the Warriors' movements closely.

But not closely enough. *Zip!* Booker shot a pass to Murdock. Murdock dribbled in and delivered a no-look side toss to Jackson. Jackson fake-pumped a shot and bounced the ball to Julian.

Julian dribbled once, twice, the ball singing against the floor and stinging against his fingertips. Then he cupped it in his left hand, guided it up with his right, and tossed in a soft jump shot from four feet away.

Fwing! The ball fell through the hoop for two points!

Applause echoed around the gym. Julian barely registered it. He was too busy racing to get back on defense.

Coach Boyd was testing out a one-three-one zone this game. Booker was in the point position, shadowing the ball carrier. Murdock, Jackson, and Will fanned out across the key. Julian took up the baseline slot, ready to join in for a double-team effort if a Raven threatened a shot from down low.

The Ravens flew down the court. They passed once, twice. A forward dribbled in as if to shoot. Booker and Murdock leaped out together to cover him. The forward backed away and passed the ball off to his center. Now Julian and Murdock surged out. Julian waved his arms madly, hoping to fluster the Raven.

Unfortunately, the Raven was as cool as a cucumber. He took a step back, shooting as he went. The ball arced like a rainbow and slid through the strings effortlessly.

The shot was so beautiful that Julian nearly whistled

out loud in admiration. *This guy is the one to watch,* he thought. *And I'm the one to watch him!*

Watch him he did, like a hawk! When the Raven center cut to the middle of the key on his team's next possession, Julian scurried to put himself in his way. When the center got the ball at the baseline, Julian rushed him, forcing him to hurry his shot. When the center drove to the hoop, Julian planted himself like a tree in his path and made him pull up short.

But despite Julian's best efforts, the Raven center racked up the points. Before the quarter was over, he had scored in the double digits!

Coach Boyd called for a time out. "Double team the guy," he told his players. "*Triple* team him if you have to! Just shut him down!"

The Warriors tried to do as the coach instructed. But the Raven center was simply too good. If they pushed him away from the hoop, he lobbed a three-pointer. If they gave him the lane, he dished in a layup. He outsmarted their triple team too, for instead of shooting, he wormed a pass through their arms to his wide-open teammates.

The Raven was just as commanding on defense too. He crashed the boards, ripping down rebounds. He stole the ball time and again. He even outjumped Julian, who was taller than he was by two inches, to slap down a shot!

But the play of the game came seconds before the end of the third quarter. Julian was taking a much-needed break on the sidelines. The Warriors were passing the ball around the key, desperately trying to find an opening to the basket. Then suddenly — *zoom*! The center flashed forward, stole the ball, and started dribbling to the other end of the court.

The Warriors and the other Ravens gave chase. But the center had a good five steps on all of them. He neared the hoop and then, amazingly, launched himself skyward and threw down a dunk just as the buzzer sounded!

"Unbelievable!" Julian shouted, clapping madly and pacing the sideline. He knew he should be upset that the Warriors were losing. But astonishment over what he had just seen trumped any disappointment he had. "Man, I would give anything to play like that!"

"Me too."

Julian hadn't realized he was so close to Paul. He stared at the other boy in surprise.

Was he hearing things — or had Paul just admitted that someone played better than he did?

21

Coach Boyd had heard Paul's comment too, it turned out. "You *do* play like him!" he sputtered to his son. "If you only could be out there right now you'd —"

"— be having just as much trouble stopping that guy as Julian is!"

Julian heard the frustration in Paul's voice. He edged away to give father and son some privacy. But he could still hear what they were saying to each other.

Now Paul shook his head. "Dad, I know you think I'm a going to be a great player. Maybe I will be, someday. But you have to see that I'm nowhere near as good as that Raven is! I may never be!"

"If you would just practice more, you would be," Coach Boyd said.

Paul let out a heavy sigh. "I practice plenty. In fact, I'd like to stop practicing so much."

"What?" Coach Boyd regarded his son with a look of disbelief. "Why?"

Julian looked over at them then. He was curious about the answer to that question too. He caught Paul's glance at Alex. Alex gave a small nod.

Go on, that nod seemed to say, *you can do it*.

"I had a lot of time to think while I was in the hospital. I realized I miss hanging out with my friends," Paul said at last. "I'm only thirteen, Dad. I'm not even in high school! I — I'm just tired of training, I guess. I want some time to have fun too."

Coach Boyd didn't say anything for a long moment. Then he spun around and strode to the scorers table. "We'll discuss this further when we get home," he said. "Right now I have a game to win."

Paul looked toward Alex again. Alex shrugged. "You tried," Julian saw him mouth. Paul nodded.

The game continued and to no one's surprise — except perhaps Coach Boyd's — the Ravens trounced the Warriors; the final score was 55 to 42. Usually, such a sound defeat would have put Julian in a foul mood. But he knew he had tried his best, and believed the other Warriors had too. This time, the other team had just been better — plain and simple.

His teammates seemed to feel the same way. Their

116

chatter was subdued around the coach, but when they were all outside in the parking lot, they began joking around with one another. Julian joined in the fun. Then he felt someone tap him on the shoulder.

He turned to see Paul standing there.

"You played a good game today," the center said.

"Thanks," Julian replied. "I'm glad you're feeling better. We need you on the court."

A slow smile spread across Paul's face. "Oh, I know you do!" He chuckled at the look on Julian's face. "Know what else? We need you on the court too. Maybe we even need both of us on at the same time. Yeah, that would've worked! If we had both teamed up against that dude today, we could have shut him down, no sweat!"

Julian grinned. "Sure! Heck, I would have even let you get between him and the hoop on that dunk!"

Paul held up his hand. "No, no! I wouldn't have dreamed of taking the honor of being mowed down by that guy away from you! You deserved it!"

The two boys burst out laughing.

"Hey, what's so funny?" Alex asked, coming over to them.

Paul grabbed him in a headlock and rubbed his knuckles over his head. "Your face, that's what's so funny!"

"I liked you better when you were lying in that hospital bed!" Alex yelped.

Julian stood to one side, laughing. The way Alex and Paul were horsing around reminded him of how he had goofed around with Grady. He felt a stab of homesickness for his old friend.

But then he realized something. He and Grady would always be friends — Barry too, and Mick and the other Tornadoes. Just because he had moved didn't mean he had to give them up. Wasn't that what all the fancy technology, like cell phones and e-mail, was for? He had a lot of ways to stay in touch; and in the meantime, he could add new friends, like Alex, Jackson, and now even Paul.

With that thought, a warm rush of happiness filled him. He turned to Alex and Paul. "Are you guys almost through pummeling each other?"

Paul gave Alex one last knuckle rub and then let him go. "Now I am. Why?"

"I was wondering if you'd like to come to my house and hang out." He gestured to the other players too. "You can all come, if you want."

"Yeah, let's have a defeat party!" Alex said, pumping his fist in the air.

"I'll come," Paul said, "but only on one condition."

"What's that, hot shot?" Alex wanted to know.

Paul pointed a finger at Julian. "That he gets rid of the rest of his Triple Chocolate Peanut Butter Death Drops! I've had enough of hospitals for this year!"

THE #1 SPORTS SERIES FOR KIDS

MATT CHRISTOPHER®

Read them all!

*Previously published as Crackerjack Halfback

All available in paperback from Little, Brown and Company

**Previously published as Pressure Play

***Previously published as Baseball Pals

Matt Christopher®

Muhammad Ali	Randy Johnson
Lance Armstrong	Michael Jordan
Kobe Bryant	Peyton and Eli Manning
Jennifer Capriati	Yao Ming
Dale Earnhardt Sr.	Shaquille O'Neal
Jeff Gordon	Albert Pujols
Ken Griffey Jr.	Jackie Robinson
Mia Hamm	Alex Rodriguez
Tony Hawk	Babe Ruth
Ichiro	Curt Schilling
LeBron James	Sammy Sosa
Derek Jeter	Tiger Woods